All the Troubles
of the World

CREATIVE CLASSICS

This wonderful short story
has passed the test of a classic:
it has lasted.
Our eyes still race eagerly as its characters
face danger, confusion or sadness.
The experience becomes a reservoir of strength.
It lies quiet in our memories until
we need a deeper wisdom
to face our own danger, confusion or sadness.
This story,
like others in the Creative Classic series,
has been rescued from the
musty, attic-world of anthologies.
It is here presented in a volume of its own,
with all the richness and dignity
a good story deserves.

ISAAC ASIMOV

All the Troubles of the World

with illustrations by
David Shannon

CREATIVE EDUCATION, INC

MANKATO, MINNESOTA

Published by Creative Education, Inc.
123 South Broad Street, Mankato, Minnesota 56001

Text copyright © 1989 by Isaac Asimov.
Illustrations copyright © 1989
by Creative Education, Inc.
Original copyright © 1958 by Headline Publications,
Inc.
Renewed © 1985 by Isaac Asimov.
Reprinted by permission of the author, Isaac Asimov.
International copyrights reserved in all countries.

Printed in the United States of America.
ISBN 0-88682-233-5

To Janet,
who's made a storybook
of my life

The greatest industry on Earth centered about Multivac—Multivac, the giant computer that had grown in fifty years until its various ramifications had filled Washington, D.C. to the suburbs and had reached out tendrils into every city and town on Earth.

An army of civil servants fed it data constantly and another army correlated and interpreted the answers it gave. A corps of engineers patrolled its interior while mines and factories consumed themselves in keeping its reserve stocks of replacement parts ever complete, ever accurate, ever satisfactory in every way.

Multivac directed Earth's economy and helped Earth's science. Most important of all, it was the central clearing house of all known facts about each individual Earthman.

And each day it was part of Multivac's duties to take the four billion sets of facts about individual human beings that filled its vitals and extrapolate them for an additional day of time. Every Corrections Department on Earth received the data appropriate to its own area of jurisdiction, and the over-all data was presented in one large piece to the Central Board of Corrections in Washington, D.C.

Bernard Gulliman was in the fourth week of his year

term as Chairman of the Central Board of Corrections and had grown casual enough to accept the morning report without being frightened by it. As usual, it was a sheaf of papers some six inches thick. He knew by now, he was not expected to read it. (No human could.) Still, it was amusing to glance through it.

There was the usual list of predictable crimes: frauds of all sorts, larcenies, riots, manslaughters, arsons.

He looked for one particular heading and felt a slight shock at finding it there at all, then another one at seeing two entries. Not one, but two. *Two* first-degree murders. He had not seen two in one day in all his term as Chairman so far.

He punched the knob of the two-way intercom and waited for the smooth face of his co-ordinator to appear on the screen.

"Ali," said Gulliman, "There are two first-degree this day. Is there any unusual problem?"

"No, sir." The dark-complexioned face with its sharp, black eyes seemed restless. "Both cases are quite low probability."

"I know that," said Gulliman. "I observed that neither probability is higher than 15 per cent. Just the same, Multivac has a reputation to maintain. It has virtually wiped out crime, and the public judges that by its record on first-degree murder which is, of course, the most spectacular crime."

Ali Othman nodded. "Yes, sir. I quite realize that."

"You also realize, I hope," Gulliman said, "that I don't want a single consummated case of it during my term. If any other crime slips through, I may allow excuses. If a first-degree murder slips through, I'll have your hide. Understand?"

"Yes, sir. The complete analyses of the two potential

murders are already at the district offices involved. The potential criminals and victims are under observation. I have rechecked the probabilities of consummation and they are already dropping."

"Very good," said Gulliman, and broke connection.

He went back to the list with an uneasy feeling that perhaps he had been overpompous.—But then, one had to be firm with these permanent civil-service personnel and make sure they didn't imagine they were running everything, including the Chairman. Particularly this Othman, who had been working with Multivac since both were considerably younger, and had a proprietary air that could be infuriating.

To Gulliman, this matter of crime was the political chance of a lifetime. So far, no Chairman had passed through his term without a murder taking place somewhere on Earth, some time. The previous Chairman had ended with a record of eight, three more (*more*, in fact) than under his predecessor.

Now Gulliman intended to have *none*. He was going to be, he had decided, the first Chairman without any murder at all anywhere on Earth during his term. After that, and the favorable publicity that would result—

He barely skimmed the rest of the report. He estimated that there were at least two thousand cases of prospective wife-beatings listed. Undoubtedly, not all would be stopped in time. Perhaps thirty percent would be consummated. But the incidence was dropping and consummations were dropping even more quickly.

Multivac had added wife-beating to its list of predictable crimes only some five years earlier and the average man was not yet accustomed to the thought that if he planned to wallop his wife, it would be known in advance. As the conviction percolated through society, women would first suffer fewer bruises and then, eventually, none.

Some husband-beatings were on the list, too, Gulliman noticed.

Ali Othman closed connections and stared at the screen from which Gulliman's jowled and balding head had departed. Then he looked across at his assistant, Rafe Leemy and said, "What do we do?"

"Don't ask me. *He's* worried about just a lousy murder or two."

"It's an awful chance trying to handle this thing on our own. Still if we tell him, he'll have a first-class fit. These elective politicians have their skins to think of, so he's bound to get in our way and make things worse."

Leemy nodded his head and put a thick lower lip between his teeth. "Trouble is, though, what if we miss out? It would just about be the end of the world, you know."

"If we miss out, who cares what happens to us? We'll just be part of the general catastrophe." Then he said in a more lively manner, "But hell, the probability is only 12.3 per cent. On anything else, except maybe murder, we'd let the probabilities rise a bit before taking any action at all. There could still be spontaneous correction."

"I wouldn't count on it," said Leemy dryly.

"I don't intend to. I was just pointing the fact out. Still, at this probability, I suggest we confine ourselves to simple observation for the moment. No one could plan a crime like this alone; there must be accomplices."

"Multivac didn't name any."

"I know. Still—" His voice trailed off.

So they stared at the details of the one crime not included on the list handed out to Gulliman; the one crime much worse than first-degree murder; the one crime never before attempted in the history of Multivac; and wondered what to do.

Ben Manners considered himself the happiest sixteen-year-old in Baltimore. This was, perhaps, doubtful. But he was certainly one of the happiest, and one of the most excited.

At least, he was one of the handful admitted to the galleries of the stadium during the swearing in of the eighteen-year-olds. His older brother was going to be sworn in so his parents had applied for spectator's tickets and they had allowed Ben to do so, too. But when Multivac choose among all the applicants, it was Ben who got the ticket.

Two years later, Ben would be sworn in himself, but watching big brother Michael now was the next best thing.

His parents had dressed him (or supervised the dressing, at any rate) with all care, as representative of the family and sent him off with numerous messages for Michael, who had left days earlier for preliminary physical and neurological examinations.

The stadium was on the outskirts of town and Ben, just bursting with self-importance, was shown to his seat. Below him, now, were rows upon rows of hundreds upon hundreds of eighteen-year-olds (boys to the right, girls to the left), all from the second district of Baltimore. At various times in the year, similar meetings are going on all over the world, but this was Baltimore, this was the important one. Down there (somewhere) was Mike, Ben's own brother.

Ben scanned the tops of heads, thinking somehow he might recognize his brother. He didn't, of course, but then a man came out on the raised platform in front of all the crowd and Ben stopped looking to listen.

The man said, "Good afternoon, swearers and guests. I am Randolph T. Hoch, in charge of the Baltimore ceremonies this year. The swearers have met me several times now during the progress of the physical and neurological portions of his examination. Most of the task is done, but the most important matter is left. The swearer himself, his personality, must go into Multivac's records.

"Each year, this requires some explanation to the young people reaching adulthood. Until now" (he turned to the young people before him and his eyes went no more to the gallery) "you have not been adult; you have not been individuals in the eyes of Multivac, except where you were especially singled out as such by your parents or your government.

"Until now, when the time for the yearly up-dating of information came, it was your parents who filled in the necessary data on you. Now the time has come for you to take over that duty yourself. It is a great honor, a great responsibility. Your parents have told us what schooling you've had, what diseases, what habits; a great many things. But now you must tell us a great deal more; your innermost thoughts; your most secret deeds.

"This is hard to do the first time, embarrassing even, but it *must* be done. Once it is done, Multivac will have a complete analysis of all of you in its files. It will understand your actions and reactions. It will even be able to guess with fair accuracy at your future actions and reactions.

"In this way, Multivac will protect you. If you are in danger of accident, it will know. If someone plans harm to you, it will know. If *you* plan harm, it will know and you will be stopped in time so that it will not be necessary to punish you.

"With its knowledge of all of you, Multivac will be able to help Earth adjust its economy and its laws for the good of all. If you have a personal problem, you may come to Multivac with it and with its knowledge of all of you, Multivac will be able to help you.

"Now you will have many forms to fill out. Think care-

fully and answer all question as accurately as you can. Do not hold back through shame or caution. No one will ever know your answers except Multivac unless it becomes necessary to learn the answers in order to protect you. And then only authorized officials of the government will know.

"It may occur to you to stretch the truth a bit here or there. Don't do this. We will find out if you do. All your answers put together form a pattern. If some answers are false, they will not fit the pattern and Multivac will discover them. If all your answers are false, there will be a distorted pattern of a type that Multivac will recognize. So you must tell the truth."

Eventually, it was all over, however; the form-filling; the ceremonies and speeches that followed. In the evening, Ben, standing tiptoe, finally spotted Michael, who was still carrying the robes he had worn in the "parade of the adults." They greeted one another with jubilation.

They shared a light supper and took the expressway home, alive and alight with the greatness of the day.

They were not prepared, then, for the sudden transition of the home-coming. It was a numbing shock to both of them to be stopped by a cold-faced young man in uniform outside their own front door; to have their papers inspected before they could enter their own house; to find their own parents sitting forlornly in the living room, the mark of tragedy on their faces.

Joseph Manners, looking much older than he had that morning, looked out of his puzzled, deep-sunken eyes at his sons (one with the robes of new adulthood still over his arm) and said, "I seem to be under house arrest."

Bernard Gulliman could not and did not read the entire report. He read only the summary and that was most gratifying, indeed.

A whole generation, it seemed, had grown up accustomed to the fact that Multivac could predict the commission of major crimes. They learned that Corrections agents would be on the scene before the crime could be committed. They found out that consummation of the crime led to inevitable punishment. Gradually, they were convinced that there was no way anyone could outsmart Multivac.

The result was, naturally, that even the intention of crime fell off. And as such intentions fell off and as Multivac's capacity was enlarged, minor crimes could be added to the list it would predict each morning, and these crimes, too, were now shrinking in incidence.

So Gulliman had ordered an analysis made (by Multivac naturally) of Multivac's capacity to turn its attention to the problem of predicting probabilities of disease incidence. Doctors might soon be alerted to individual patients who might grow diabetic in the course of the next year, or suffer an attack of tuberculosis or grow a cancer.

An ounce of prevention—

And the report was a favorable one!

After that, the roster of the day's possible crimes arrived and there was not a first-degree murder on the list.

Gulliman put in an intercom call to Ali Othman in high good humor. "Othman, how do the numbers of crimes in the daily list of the past week average compared with those in my first week as Chairman?"

It had gone down, it turned out, by 8 per cent and Gulliman was happy indeed. No fault of his own, of course, but the electorate would not know that. He blessed his luck that had come in at the right time, at the very climax of Multivac, when disease, too, could be placed under its all-embracing and protecting knowledge.

Gulliman would prosper by this.

Othman shrugged his shoulders. "Well, he's happy,"

"When do we break the bubble?" said Leemy. "Putting Manners under observation just raised the probabilities and house arrest gave it another boost."

"Don't I know it?" said Othman peevishly. "What I don't know is why."

"Accomplices, maybe, like you said. With Manners in trouble, the rest have to strike at once or be lost."

"Just the other way around. With our hand on one, the rest would scatter for safety and disappear. Besides, why aren't the accomplices named by Multivac?"

"Well, then, do we tell Gulliman?"

"No, not yet. The probability is still only 17.3 per cent. Let's get a bit more drastic first."

Elizabeth Manners said to her younger son, "You go to your room, Ben."

"But what's it all about, Mom?" asked Ben, voice breaking at this strange ending to what had been a glorious day.

"Please!"

He left reluctantly, passing through the door to the stairway, walking up it noisily and down again quietly.

And Mike Manners, the older son, the new-minted adult and the hope of the family, said in a voice and tone that mirrored his brother's, "What's it all about?"

Joe Manners said, "As heaven is my witness, son, I don't know. I haven't done anything."

"Well, sure you haven't done anything." Mike looked at his small-boned, mild-mannered father in wonder. "They must be here because you're *thinking* of doing something."

"I'm not."

Mrs. Manners broke in angrily. "How can he be thinking of doing something worth all—all this." She cast her arm about, in a gesture toward the enclosing shell of government men about the house. "When I was a little girl, I remember the father of a friend of mine was working in a bank, and they once called him up and said to leave the money alone and he did. It was fifty thousand dollars. He hadn't really taken it. He was just thinking about taking it. They didn't keep those things as quiet in those days as they do now; the story got out. That's how I know about it.

"But I mean," she went on, rubbing her plump hands slowly together, "that was fifty thousand dollars; fifty— thousand—dollars. Yet all they did was call him; one phone call. What could your father be planning that would make it worth having a dozen men come down and close off the house?"

Joe Manners said, eyes filled with pain, "I am planning no crime, not even the smallest. I swear it."

Mike, filled with the conscious wisdom of a new adult, said, "Maybe it's something subconscious, Pop. Some resentment against your supervisor."

"So that I would want to kill him? No!"

"Won't they tell you what it is, Pop?"

His mother interrupted again, "No, they won't. We've asked. I said they were ruining our standing in the com-

munity just being here. The least they could do is tell us what it's all about so we could fight it, so we could explain."

"And they wouldn't?"

"They wouldn't."

Mike stood with his legs spread apart and his hands deep in his pockets. He said, troubled, "Gee, Mom, Multivac doesn't make mistakes.

His father pounded his fist helplessly on the arm of the sofa. "I tell you I'm not planning any crime."

The door opened without a knock and a man in uniform walked in with sharp, self-possessed stride. His face had a glazed, official appearance. He said, "Are you Joseph Manners?"

Joe Manners rose to his feet. "Yes. Now what is it you want of me?"

"Joseph Manners, I place you under arrest by order of

the government," and curtly he showed his identification as a Corrections officer. "I must ask you to come with me."

"For what reason? What have I done?"

"I am not at liberty to discuss that."

"But I can't be arrested just for planning a crime even if I were doing that. To be arrested I must actually have *done* something. You can't arrest me otherwise. It's against the law."

The officer was impervious to the logic. "You will have to come with me."

Mrs. Manners shrieked and fell on the couch, weeping hysterically. Joseph Manners could not bring himself to violate the code drilled into him all his life by actually resisting an officer, but he hung back at least, forcing the Corrections officer to use muscular power to drag him forward.

And Manners called out as he went, "But tell me what it is. Just tell me. If I *knew*—Is it murder? Am I supposed to be planning murder?"

The door closed behind him and Mike Manners, white-faced and suddenly feeling not the least bit adult, stared first at the door, then at his weeping mother.

Ben Manners, behind the door and suddenly feeling quite adult, pressed his lips tightly together and thought he knew exactly what do do.

If Multivac took away, Multivac could also give. Ben had been at the ceremonies that very day. He had heard this man, Randolph Hoch, speak of Multivac and all that Multivac could do. It could direct the government and it could also unbend and help out some plain person who came to it for help.

Anyone could ask help of Multivac and anyone meant Ben. Neither his mother nor Mike were in any condition to stop him now, and he had some money left of the amount

they had given him for his great outing that day. If after-
ward they found him gone and worried about it, that
couldn't be helped. Right now, his first loyalty was to his
father.

He ran out the back way and the officer at the door cast
a glance at his papers and let him go.

Harold Quimby handled the complaints department of
the Baltimore substation of Multivac. He considered
himself to be a member of that branch of the civil service
that was most important of all. In some ways, he may have
been right, and those who heard him discuss the matter
would have had to be made of iron not to feel impressed.

For one thing, Quimby would say, Multivac was essen-
tially an invader of privacy. In the past fifty years, mankind had had to acknowledge that its thoughts and im-
pulses were no longer secret, that it owned no inner recess
where anything could be hidden. And mankind had to have
something in return.

Of course, it got prosperity, peace, and safety, but that
was abstract. Each man and woman needed something personal as his or her own reward for surrendering privacy,
and each one got it. Within reach of every human being as
a Multivac station with circuits into which he could freely
enter his own problems and questions without control or
hindrance, and from which, in a matter of minutes, he
could receive answers.

At any given moment, five million individual circuits
among the quadrillion or more within Multivac might be
involved in this question-and-answer program. The answers might not always be certain, but they were the best
available, and every questioner *knew* the answer to be the
best available and had faith in it. That was what counted.

And now an anxious sixteen-year-old had moved slowly up the waiting line of men and women (each in that line illuminated by a different mixture of hope with fear or anxiety or even anguish—always with hope predominating as the person stepped nearer and nearer to Multivac).

Without looking up, Quimby took the filled-out form being handed him and said, "Booth 5-B."

Ben said, "How do I ask the question, sir?"

Quimby looked up then, with a bit of surprise. Preadults did not generally make use of the service. He said kindly, "Have you ever done this before, son?"

"No, sir."

Quimby pointed to the model on his desk. "You use this. You see how it works? Just like a typewriter. Don't you try to write or print anything by hand. Just use the machine. Now you take booth 5-B, and if you need help, just press the red button and someone will come. Down that aisle, son, on the right."

He watched the youngster go down the aisle and out of view and smiled. No one was ever turned away from Multivac. Of course, there was always a certain percentage of trivia: people who asked personal questions about their neighbors or obscene questions about prominent personalities; college youths trying to outguess their professors or thinking it clever to stump Multivac by asking it Russell's class-of-all-classes paradox and so on.

Multivac could take care of that. It needed no help.

Besides, each question and answer was filed and formed but another item in the fact assembly for each individual. Even the most trivial question and the most impertinent, insofar as it reflected the personality of the questioner, helped humanity by helping Multivac know about humanity.

Quimby turned his attention to the next person in line, a middle-aged woman, gaunt and angular, with the look of trouble in her eye.

Ali Othman strode the length of his office, his heels thumping desperately on the carpet. "The probability still goes up. It's 22.4 per cent now. Damnation! We have Joseph Manners under actual arrest and it still goes up." He was perspiring freely.

Leemy turned away from the telephone. "No confession yet. He's under Psychic Probing and there is no sign of crime. He may be telling the truth."

Othman said, "Is Multivac crazy then?"

Another phone sprang to life. Othman closed connections quickly, glad of the interruption. A Corrections officer's face came to life in the screen. The officer said, "Sir, are there any new directions as to Manners' family? Are they to be allowed to come and go as they have been?"

"What do you mean, as they have been?"

"The original instructions were for the house arrest of Joseph Manners. Nothing was said of the rest of the family, sir."

"Well, extend it to the rest of the family until you are informed otherwise."

"Sir, that is the point. The mother and older son are demanding information about the younger son. The younger son is gone and they claim he is in custody and wish to go to headquarters to inquire about it."

Othman frowned and said in almost a whisper, "Younger son? How young?"

"Sixteen, sir," said the officer.

"Sixteen and he's gone. Don't you know where?"

"He was allowed to leave, sir. There were no orders to hold him."

"Hold the line. Don't move." Othman put the line into suspension, then clutched at his coal-black hair with both hands and shrieked, "Fool! Fool! Fool!"

Leemy was startled. "What the hell?"

"The man has a sixteen-year-old-son," choked out Othman. "A sixteen-year-old is not an adult and he is not filed independently in Multivac, but only as part of his father's file." He glared at Leemy. "Doesn't everyone know that until eighteen a youngster does not file his own reports with Multivac but that his father does it for him? Don't I know it? Don't you?"

"You mean Multivac didn't mean Joe Manners?" said Leemy.

"Multivac meant his minor son, and the youngster is gone now. With officers three deep around the house, he calmly walks out and goes on you know what errand."

He whirled to the telephone circuit to which the Corrections officer still clung, the minute break having given Othman just time enough to collect himself and to assume a cool and self-possessed mien. (It would never have done to throw a fit before the eyes of the officer, however much good it did in purging his spleen.)

He said, "Officer, locate the younger son who has disappeared. Take every man you have, if necessary. Take every man available in the district, if necessary. I shall give the appropriate orders. You must find that boy at all costs."

"Yes, sir."

Connection was broken. Othman said, "Have another

rundown on the probabilities, Leemy."

Five minutes later, Leemy said, "It's down to 19.6 per cent. It's *down*."

Othman drew a long breath. "We're on the right track at last."

Ben Manners sat in Booth 5-B and punched out slowly, "My name is Benjamin Manners, number MB-71833412. My father, Joseph Manners, has been arrested but we don't know what crime he is planning. Is there any way we can help him?"

He sat and waited. He might be only sixteen but he was old enough to know that somewhere those words were being whirled into the most complex structure ever conceived by man; that a trillion facts would blend and co-ordinate into a whole, and that from that whole, Multivac would abstract the best help.

The machine clicked and a card emerged. It had an answer on it, a long answer. It began, "Take the expressway to Washington, D.C. at once. Get off at the Connecticut Avenue stop. You will find a special exit, labeled 'Multivac' with a guard. Inform the guard you are special courier for Dr. Trumbull and he will let you enter.

"You will be in a corridor. Proceed along it till you reach a small door labeled 'Interior.' Enter and say to the men inside, 'Message for Doctor Trumbull.' You will be allowed to pass. Proceed on—"

It went on in this fashion. Ben could not see the application to his question, but he had complete faith in Multivac. He left at a run, heading for the expressway to Washington.

The Corrections officers traced Ben Manners to the Baltimore station an hour after he had left. A shocked Harold Quimby found himself flabbergasted at the number and

importance of the men who had focused on him in the
search for a sixteen-year-old.

"Yes, a boy," he said, "but I don't know where he went to
after he was through here. I had no way of knowing that
anyone was looking for him. We accept all comers here.
Yes, I can get the record of the question and answer."

They looked at the record and televised it to Central
Headquarters at once.

Othman read it through, turned up his eyes, and collapsed. They brought him to almost at once. He said to
Leemy weakly, "Have them catch that boy. And have a
copy of Multivac's answer made out for me. There's no way
any more, no way out. I must see Gulliman now."

Bernard Gulliman had never seen Ali Othman as much
as perturbed before, and watching the co-ordinator's wild
eyes now sent a trickle of ice water down his spine.

He stammered. "What do you mean, Othman? What do
you mean worse than murder?"

"Much worse than just murder."

Gulliman was quite pale. "Do you mean assassination of
a high government official?" (It did cross his mind that he
himself—)

Othman nodded. "Not just a government official. *The*
government official.

"The *Secretary-General*?" Gulliman said in an appalled
whisper.

"More than that, even. Much more. We deal with a plan
to assassinate Multivac!"

"WHAT!"

"For the first time in the history of Multivac, the computer came up with the report that it itself was in danger."

"Why was I not at once informed?"

Othman half-truthed out of it. "The matter was so un-

precedented, sir, that we explored the situation first before
daring to put it on official record."

"But Multivac has been saved, of course? It's been
saved?"

"The probabilities of harm have declined to under 4 percent. I am waiting for the report now."

"Message for Dr. Trumbull," said Ben Manners to the
man on the high stool, working carefully on what looked
like the controls of a stratojet cruiser, enormously magni-
fied.

"Sure, Jim," said the man. "Go ahead."

Ben looked at his instructions and hurried on. Eventually, he would find a tiny control lever which he was to
shift to a DOWN position at a moment when a certain in-
dicator spot would light up red.

He heard an agitated voice behind him, then another,
and suddenly, two men had him by his elbows. His feet
were lifted off the floor.

One man said, "Come with us, boy."

Ali Othman's face did not noticeably lighten at the
news, even though Gulliman said with great relief,
"If we have the boy, then Multivac is safe."

"For the moment."

Gulliman put a trembling hand to his forehead. "What a
half hour I've had. Can you imagine what the destruction
of Multivac for even a short time would mean. The government would have collapsed; the economy broken down. It
would have meant devastation worse—" His head snapped
up, "What do you mean *for the moment?*"

The boy, this Ben Manners, had no intention of doing
harm. He and his family must be released and compensa-
tion for false imprisonment given them. He was only fol-

lowing Multivac's instructions in order to help his father and it's done that. His father is free now."

"Do you mean Multivac ordered the boy to pull a lever under circumstances that would burn out enough circuits to require a month's repair work? You mean Multivac would suggest its own destruction for the comfort of one man?"

"It's worse than that, sir. Multivac not only gave those instructions but selected the Manners family in the first place because Ben Manners looked exactly like one of Dr. Trumbull's pages so that he could get into Multivac without being stopped."

"What do you mean the family was selected?"

"Well, the boy would never have gone to ask the question if his father had not been arrested. His father would never have been arrested if Multivac had not blamed him for planning the destruction of Multivac. Multivac's own action started the chain of events that almost led to Multivac's destruction."

"But there's no sense to that," Gulliman said in a pleading voice. He felt small and helpless and he was virtually on his knees, begging this Othman, this man who had spent nearly a lifetime with Multivac, to reassure him.

Othman did not do so. He said, "This is Multivac's first attempt along this line as far as I know. In some ways, it planned well. It chose the right family. It carefully did not distinguish between father and son to send us off the track. It was still an amateur at the game, though. It could not overcome its own instructions that led it to report the probability of its own destruction as increasing with every step we took down the wrong road. It could not avoid recording the answer it gave the youngster. With further practice, it will probably learn deceit. It will learn to hide certain facts, fail to record certain others. From

now on, every instruction it gives may have the seeds in it of its own destruction. We will never know. And however careful we are, eventually Multivac will succeed. I think, Mr. Gulliman, you will be the last Chairman of this organization."

Gulliman pounded his desk in fury. "But why, why, why? Damn you, why? What is wrong with it? Can't it be fixed?"

"I don't think so," said Othman, in soft despair. "I've never thought about this before. I've never had the occasion to until this happened, but now that I think of it, it seems to me we have reached the end of the road because Multivac is too good. Multivac has grown so complicated, its reactions are no longer those of a machine, but those of a living thing."

"You're mad, but even so?"

"For fifty years and more we have been loading humanity's troubles on Multivac, on this living thing. We've asked it to care for us, all together and each individually. We've asked it to take all our secrets into itself; we've asked it to absorb our evil and guard us against it. Each of us brings his troubles to it, adding his bit to the burden. Now we are planning to load the burden of human disease on Multivac, too."

Othman paused a moment, then burst out, "Mr. Gulliman, Multivac bears all the troubles of the world on its shoulders and it is tired."

"Madness. Midsummer madness," muttered Gulliman.

"Then let me show you something. Let me put it to the test. May I have permission to use the Multivac circuit line here in your office?"

"Why?"

"To ask it a question no one has ever asked Multivac before?"

"Will you do it harm?" asked Gulliman in quick alarm.

"No. But it will tell us what we want to know."

The Chairman hestitated a trifle. Then he said, "Go ahead."

Othman used the instrument on Gulliman's desk. His fingers punched out the question with deft strokes: "Multivac, what do you yourself want more than anything else?"

The moment between question and answer lengthened unbearably, but neither Othman nor Gulliman breathed.

And there was a clicking and a card popped out. It was a small card. On it, in precise letters, was the answer:

"I want to die."

*   *   *

Little did Judah and Anna Asimov know, in 1923, when they immigrated to the United States from Russia, that their son, Isaac, would become one of the most prolific and respected writers of our time. When the Asimov family arrived in the United States, they settled in Brooklyn, where they opened a candy store.

At the age of nine, Isaac began working in his parents' store after school. It was then he discovered the magic inside the science fiction magazines which the candy store sold. Being very strict, Isaac's father only consented to Isaac reading these magazines because he believed they were about science, and he wanted his son to one day be a doctor.

Being an excellent student, Isaac graduated from high school when he was only fifteen years old. He went directly on to Columbia University where he chose chemistry as his pre-med course of study. Asimov's interest in writing had been building for many years, and he was excited when he sold his first science fiction story while still in college. After graduation, he went on to obtain his M.A. in chemistry from Columbia before serving as a Naval chemist in World War II. Asimov returned from the war and began working on his Ph.D., also in chemistry from Columbia University, which he finished in 1948. Asimov had continued writing science fiction this whole time when, in 1949, he was asked to teach biochemistry at Boston University. Enjoying teaching and lecturing very much, Asimov accepted the position.

Asimov continued to write during his tenure at the university, but found it increasingly difficult to spend the necessary time on his writing and teaching. In 1958, Asimov decided to leave Boston Uni-

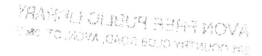

versity and devote himself to writing full-time. By then, Asimov had broadened his writing to include non-fiction, and he was developing a reputation for being a standout author of science texts for young people and laymen. He has continued, since that time, to produce a vast body of material which ranges from science fiction, to science fact, to history to Shakespeare. When asked how he could possibly write on so many diverse subjects, Asimov explained that his purpose is not to become an expert on any one thing, but rather, to learn what is necessary of a topic to discuss it intelligently.

One area in which Asimov is universally considered expert is robotics. Asimov developed, in his 1959 novel, I, ROBOT, the three laws of robotics. They are: (1) A robot may not injure a human being, or through inaction allow a human being to come to harm, (2) a robot must obey the orders given it by human beings except where such orders would conflict with the first law, and (3) a robot must protect its own existence as long as such protection does not conflict with the first or second law. Although written nearly forty years ago, it is believed these laws will be incorporated into robots of the future.

Asimov has also established himself as a first-rate lecturer. He enjoys it very much and lectures frequently on the East coast. Asimov considers himself a "ham" and can speak for hours in front of a responsive audience.

In the past, in the present, and most certainly in the future, Isaac Asimov is a name which is widely known and highly respected. It is a name which graces many literary genres and lecture halls. It is a name which represents a man who can, above all, communicate on many levels, about many things, with many people.

About the Artist

David Shannon graduated from Art Center College of Design in 1983 and now lives in New York City. His work has appeared in many publications including Time, The New York Times, *and* Rolling Stone, *as well as on a poster for a Broadway play.*

ART DIRECTION AND DESIGN
Tilman Reitzle

COLOR SEPARATIONS
Colour Graphics—Minneapolis, Minnesota

BIOGRAPHY
Cindy Fitterer Klingel

TYPESETTING
Trufont Typographers, Inc.—Hicksville, New York

PRINTING
Worzalla Publishing Co.—Stevens Point, Wisconsin

ALSO BY

ISAAC ASIMOV

Robbie

Sally

Franchise

It's Such a Beautiful Day

Published by Creative Education